# Kudzu Chaos

# Kudzu Chaos

**Written by**
**Jennifer Holloway Lambe**

**Illustrated by**
**Alison Davis Lyne**

PELICAN PUBLISHING COMPANY
Gretna 2003

*To Tim, Sydney, Mom, and Dad.*
*I love you all and appreciate your unwavering love and support!*

*The word "Pelican" and the depiction of a pelican are trademarks*
*of Pelican Publishing Company, Inc., and are registered*
*in the U.S. Patent and Trademark Office.*

**Library of Congress Cataloging-in-Publication Data**

Lambe, Jennifer Holloway.
  Kudzu chaos / by Jennifer Holloway Lambe ; illustrated by Alison Davis
Lyne.
    p. cm.
Summary: When rampant kudzu vines threaten the sleepy town of Red Mud
Flats, one brave soul ventures into the vines in search of Kudzu Katie, who
helps the townspeople find a way to turn the problem into an asset.
  ISBN 1-58980-157-1 (hardcover : alk. paper)
[1. Kudzu—Fiction. 2. City and town life—Fiction. 3. Southern States—
Fiction.] I. Lyne, Alison Davis, ill. II. Title.
  PZ7.L1677Ku 2003
  [E]—dc21
                                2003009061

Printed in Korea
Published by Pelican Publishing Company, Inc.
1000 Burmaster Street, Gretna, Louisiana 70053

# KUDZU CHAOS

Red Mud Flats was a sleepy little town—until the kudzu chaos. We're still trying to figure out what happened. Some folks say it was the heavy rains; others think it was the beginning of the end of time. We may never solve the mystery, but kudzu changed our lives forever.

Kudzu creeps across barns and winds around trees.
It covers anything in its path.

Old-timers say if you stand in one spot too long, kudzu will grow across your feet.

Our lives were normal until one summer night when the kudzu grew at an incredible rate. We went to sleep after an ordinary day, but the next morning we woke up to kudzu chaos. We had always lived with kudzu, but that night it took over.

It was like a big, green blanket thrown over the town. It grew across the streets and covered the cars. It grew across the roof of our house and down our chimney. Up and down the street, people looked out their windows and doors and wondered what to do about the kudzu.

We were shut off from the world. Soon our food began to run out. My mother said if a miracle didn't happen soon, we would have to eat the kudzu. Yuck!

The mayor called a town meeting.

"Citizens of Red Mud Flats," he cried, "we must break the tyranny of this kudzu!" (Our mayor always talked that way. It sounded like English, but no one understood him.) "We need a plan."

"What about Kudzu Katie? Maybe she could help us," I suggested.
"Bobby Lee, that's a spectacular idea! A fearless volunteer can
bring her here. She will deliver us from this botanical siege. Now,
who will go?"

I looked around—no hands. The mayor needed someone, so I volunteered. People clapped. My mother cried. My father patted my shoulder and said he was proud. Everyone agreed I was the best choice because I was experienced—I had played in the kudzu for years.

I left the next morning. The forest was spooky. Kudzu hung from the trees like green spaghetti. As I walked, I tried to remember the stories I'd heard about Kudzu Katie.

I'd never seen her, but I'd heard she was a hillbilly who lived in the woods and grew kudzu on purpose! I'd also heard she had a book of recipes for magic spells and kudzu leaves were the main ingredient.

Near sundown, I saw a small cottage with a big kudzu garden. A woman wearing a faded dress and a braided kudzu belt was working in the garden. She wore a straw hat with kudzu vines hanging down the sides like locks of green hair. She looked strange, but her face was kind. She had to be Kudzu Katie. I gathered my courage and entered her garden, where I told her of our kudzu chaos.

"Your town has a kudzu problem. Hmmm. I think the only kudzu problem is not enough kudzu, but I might be able to help," she said. "It's too late to leave tonight. Come inside and have supper. I'm cooking a kudzu casserole and biscuits with kudzu-blossom jelly."

I politely declined her offer. But soon my stomach started growling and the food did smell good.

Eating even kudzu seemed better than starving, so I held my nose and took a bite. To my surprise, the food was delicious! I even had seconds.

The next morning we started for town. By afternoon, we reached Red Mud Flats. As we climbed over the vines covering Main Street, Katie stopped and picked several leaves. She ate one and rolled her eyes as if she had just tasted the sweetest Georgia peach.

At the town square, she sat on a thick vine and began reading an old book she pulled from her bag. People came out to the square to get a closer look.

"What is she perusing?" the mayor whispered. "Is it the instructions for ridding our fair city of this terrible plague? Can she perform a magnificent miracle that will save our village?"

I shrugged my shoulders.

Katie read as the townspeople gathered around the square. They were watching and waiting for the magic. At sunset, she asked for a flashlight and read through the night.

At dawn, she closed the book and looked at our hopeful faces. "I'm sorry, neighbors. There's no magic to reverse your problem. You must learn to live with the kudzu."

The crowd started to mumble. The mumble turned into a *grumble*. The *grumble* grew to a **rumble.** And the **rumble** became a **ROAR!**

Standing below the statue of our founding father, Beauregard Fillimore Cotton Lewis, Katie raised her hands and cried, "Wait . . . you don't understand! You don't have to live like this," she said, gesturing at the town around her. "For whatever reason, kudzu grows abundantly here. Use it to your advantage."

Again, the crowd started to mumble. The mumble turned into a *grumble*. The *grumble* grew to a **rumble.** And the **rumble** became a **ROAR!**

"Let her talk!" I yelled, jumping up next to the statue. "We've asked for help so let's listen."

The crowd hushed and she told her plan.

"Trim the kudzu from your streets and yards, but save the cuttings. Use large, strong vines like this one for making furniture. Weave smaller vines into baskets and rugs. Use the tender leaves for cooking and baking."

"What will we do with the things we make?" asked the pharmacist.

"Sell your kudzu crafts to tourists," said Katie. "Tourists love souvenirs!"

The crowd was silent. Then they started to mumble. The mumble turned into a *hum*. The *hum* grew to a **whoop.** And the **whoop** became a **HOLLER!**

"This will put Red Mud Flats on the map!" cried the minister.

"People will come from everywhere to buy our furniture and baskets!" shouted the sheriff.

"We can make kudzu bread, kudzu jelly, kudzu pudding, and even kudzu ice cream," said the local chef.

The whole town pitched in and made the plan a success. Red Mud Flats became famous for its kudzu crafts.

The town elected Katie as mayor. We built a statue of her on the town square, next to Beauregard Fillimore Cotton Lewis. It seemed fitting since Beauregard started our town and Katie saved it. Mayor Katie appointed me as her official assistant. Mostly that means I help her tend her kudzu garden.

Red Mud Flats survived the kudzu chaos and became a better town. Who could have guessed that the same vine we considered a curse is now a celebrated crop?

Life is really all about how you look at things.

*Kudzu-covered objects*

*Kudzu basket (crafts created by artist Regina Hines, Ball Ground, Ga.)*

*Kudzu birdhouse*

*Kudzu angel*

## Author's Note

*Kudzu Chaos* was inspired by a real plant. Kudzu was introduced to America in 1876 at the United States Centennial Exposition. It was originally presented as a decorative garden plant. In the 1930s, the U.S. Department of Agriculture planted thousands of kudzu seedlings along roads and hillsides to prevent erosion, and kudzu has had a stranglehold on the South ever since.

Almost anywhere, you can see the vine growing on utility poles, fences, trees, and anything else that doesn't move. Currently, it covers more than two million acres of forestland. The vine is difficult to eliminate once it has taken root and it grows at an amazing rate. At peak growing season, kudzu can grow more than a foot a day! If the world continues to get warmer, scientists say that by 2030 the vine could spread as far north as the Great Lakes.

People have found creative ways to manage kudzu. The leaves and shoots are used in cooking and the vines are used to make furniture, baskets, and handmade paper.